This edition published by Parragon Books Ltd in 2014
and distributed by

Parragon Inc.
440 Park Avenue South, 13th Floor
New York, NY 10016
www.parragon.com

Written by Frances Prior-Reeves
Designed by Talking Design
Illustrations by Eleanor Carter

ISBN 978-1-4723-4051-1

Printed in China

Live, Imagine, Draw

PaRragon

Bath · New York · Cologne · Melbourne · Delhi
Hong Kong · Shenzhen · Singapore · Amsterdam

"ART ENA
TO FIND OU
LOSE OURSE
SAME

Thomas

BLES US
RSELVES AND
LVES AT THE
TIME."

Merton.

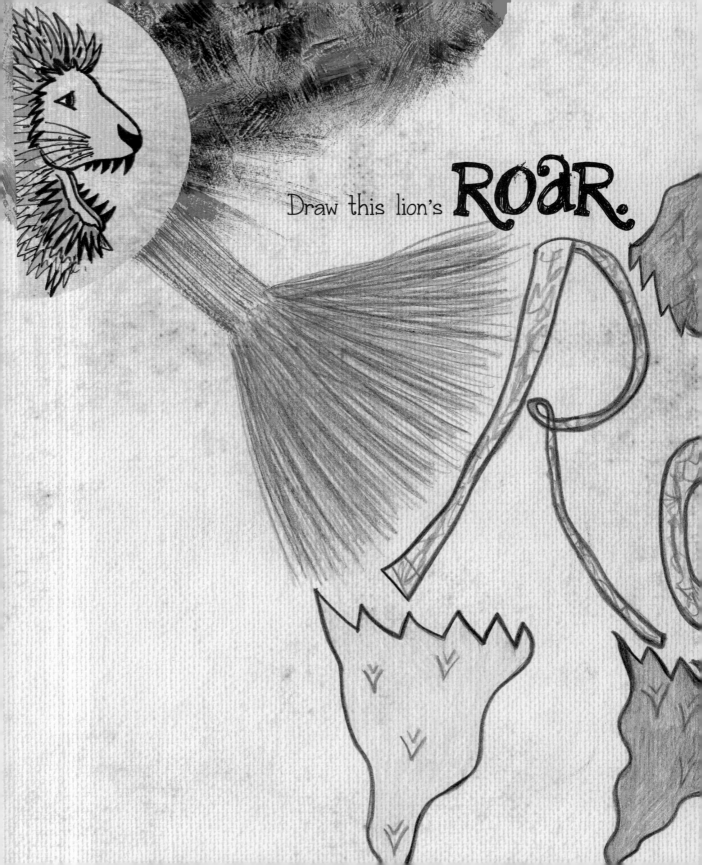

Draw this lion's **ROAR.**

FILL this page with as

much **color** as you can.

Shade
this page using only a pencil.

FREE
DRAWING
SPACE.

Think outside the **box.**

Draw your ideas
overflowing
from this box.

Add some HATS
to these animals.

Design your own *everlasting knot.*

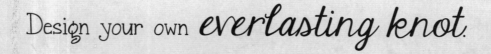

Draw the same object in **two dimensions** and then in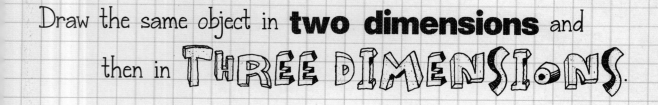

Draw your
favorite season.

Draw your LEAST FAVORITE SEASON.

"The aim
represent not
appearance
their inward

of art is to
the outward
of things, but
significance."

˵Aristotle.

Add bodies to these eyes.

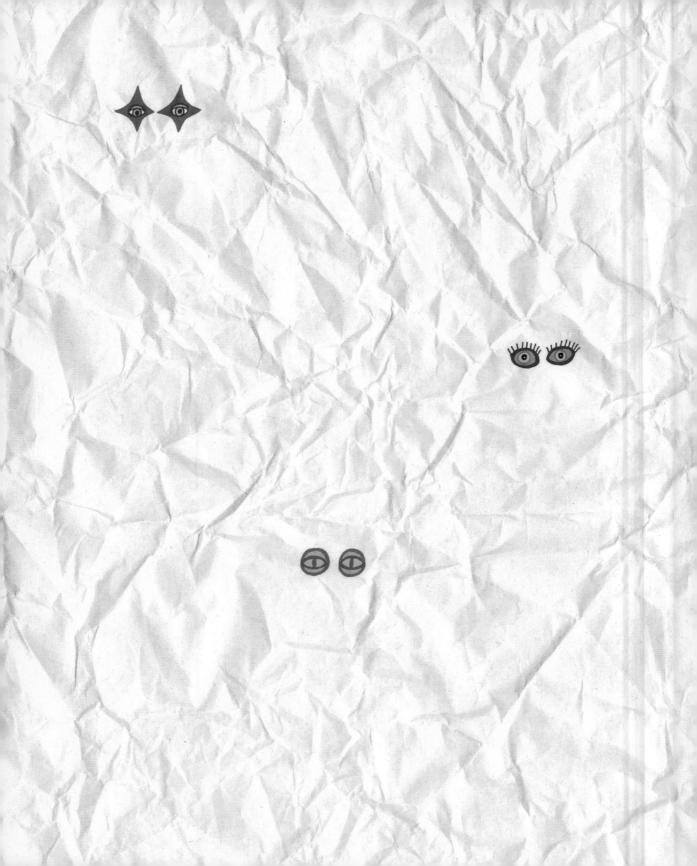

What does the color red look like when it's jealous?

What does the
color yellow look
like when it's **excited?**

Draw a ZIGZAG
chasing a curve.

Draw a CIRCLE eating a square.

Create!

Draw some **caterpillars** in this meadow.

Draw some *butterflies* flying above it.

Dream

CREATE

love

cut

PASTE

MAKE

believe

PRACTICE

write

DO

DRAW

paint

find

...inspiration.

Draw your *mood*
using a single color.

Design some **masquerade** masks.

Draw your **favorite show** on this stage.

"Every was an am

Ralph Waldo

artist
first
ateur. "'

Emerson.

Imagine!

Fill these pages with LIGHTNING.

Fill these pages with
RED creatures.

Without taking your *pen off of the page,* draw what is outside your window.

Draw something **DANGEROUS.**

UNVEIL A
PICTURE.

Shade!

Color these **patterns** without using the same color twice.

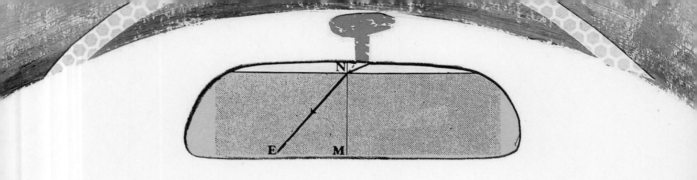

Draw the view from this
car window.

Draw the view of that
same car from a distance.

Fill this page with things that SWIM.

Fill this page with things that *fly.*

Draw something that is
EXTINCT.

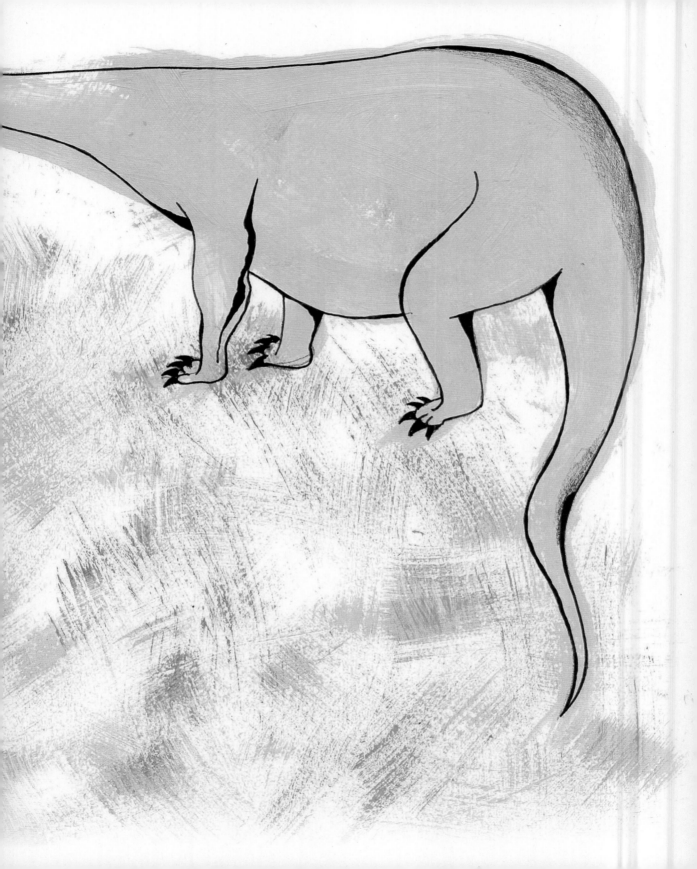

Write a list of words about **wind.**

Blow those words into a
drawing of a windy day.

Draw a **PREDATOR**
chasing its prey.

Draw your *journey.*

Draw a PORTRAIT of yourself at your most creative.

Draw a PORTRAIT of yourself at your least creative.

COLOR OUTSIDE THE LINES!

Fill this page with **orange** objects.

Pick a color.
Look around and draw what you
see that is that color.

Don't think,
just draw.

Draw a war between
green and RED.

Add some *plants* to this vegetable patch.

"A #2 PENCIL AND A DREAM

Joyce Meyer.

CAN TAKE YOU ANYWHERE. "

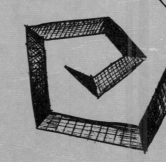

Draw squares *spiraling.*

Draw hearts
spinning.

Draw a **DREAM.**

IDEAS!

Draw an *animal* from the zoo behind these bars.

Draw the same animal in its
natural habitat.

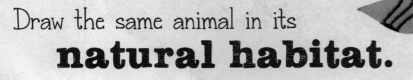

Draw a **Landslide.**

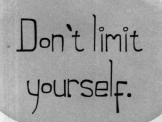

Draw the reflection in a ...

SPOON,

doorknob,

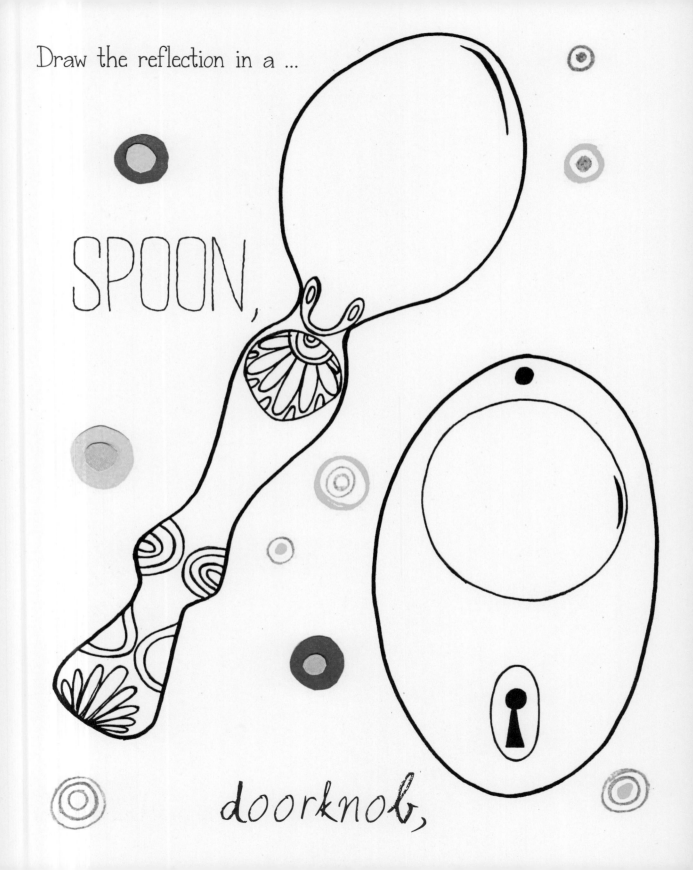

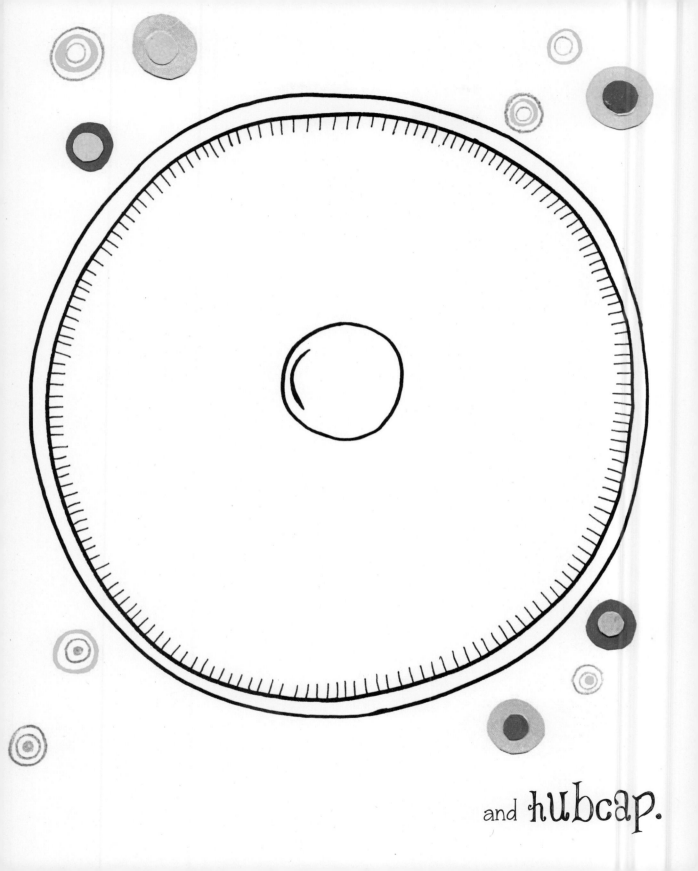

and hUbcap.

Draw the perfect weather.

Draw the eye of
the STORM.

Draw something

Draw the **songs** or **music** coming from around this campfire.

Draw a landscape.

Now, draw the same
view after a *snowfall*.

Fill this whale shape with BLUE creatures.

Draw the inside of this

PITCH-BLACK CAVE.

Draw an
ancient doorway.

Draw what's BEHIND this door.

Draw a *dreamy* color.

Draw a petrified color.

Draw a **MACHO** color.

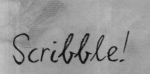
Scribble!

Draw something that is *small*,
but so that it fills this page.

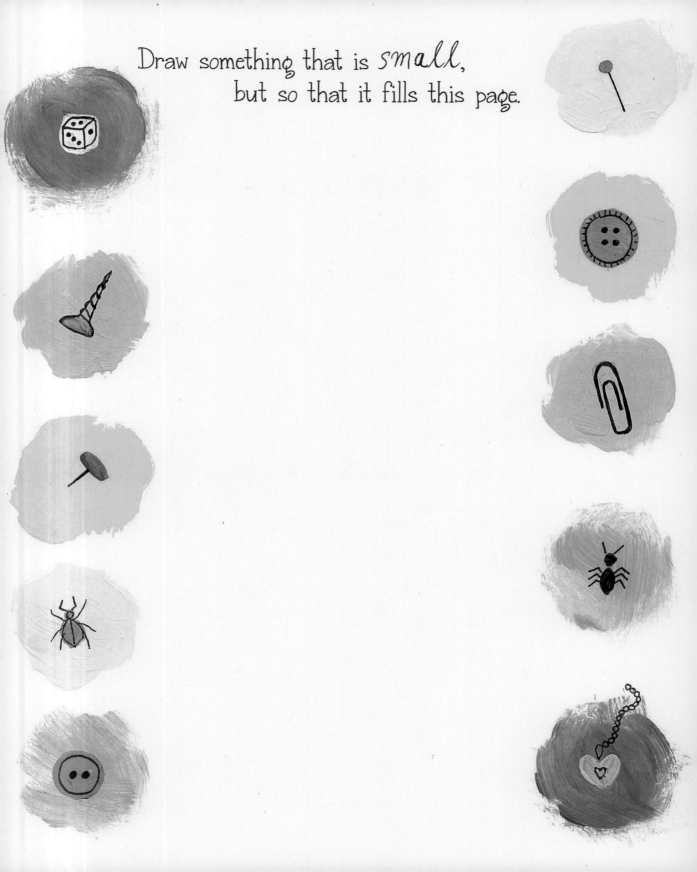

"To make pictures big is to make them more powerful."

Robert Mapplethorpe.

Draw a *cover design* for your all-time favorite book.

Draw a cover design for your least favorite book.

If you're given ruled paper, write the other way.

Write a list of words about color.

Can you make those words into an *abstract* piece of art?

Draw what is in this SUITCASE.

Draw *pink* and **black** in love.

Draw an argument between **yellow** and ORANGE.

Hannah

Draw *burgundy* and
TURQUOISE dancing and spinning.

Draw an **aerial view** of where you are.

Hannah

Looking up

Hannah

Looking down

♡

Draw!

A BROWN

COW!!

Hannah

A weird

lookin pig

Hannah

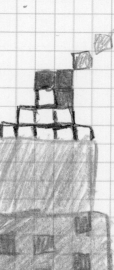

Hannah

Create a **mosaic** using this graph paper.

Now try again using a **smaller** grid.

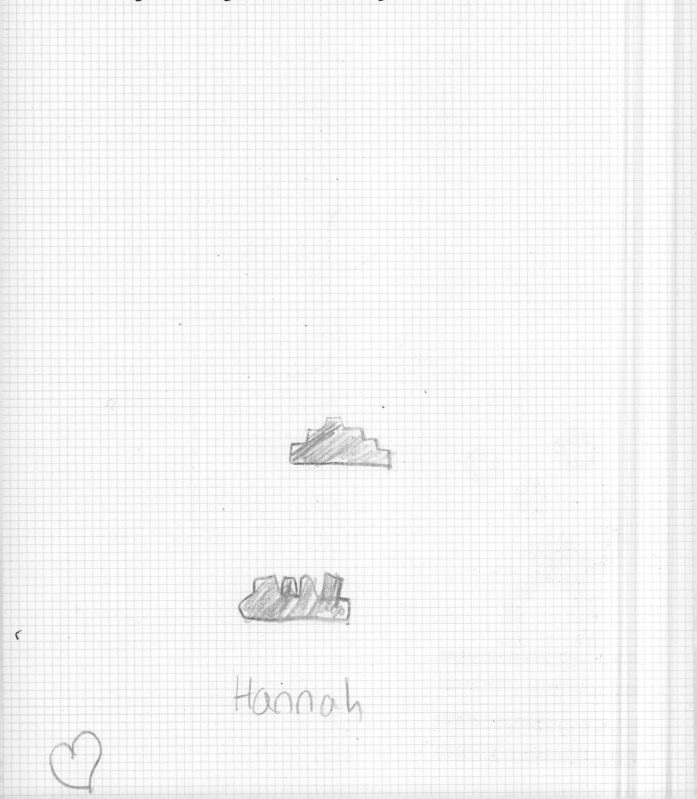

Hannah

Draw something *scared-*

Aanah

Draw something SCARY.

Personalize these pages.

Hannah

L Love
O a-mazing
V Very kind
E Everything that x2 happens
Y I will still LOVE you.

#PROUY

color

line

shape

form

texture

space

value

emphasis

balance

pattern

contrast

proportion

variety

Draw something OLD.

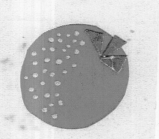

Draw something *soft.*

Draw something **hard.**

Draw a *rainbow scene* in black and white.

Draw a gray, rainy day using fluorescent colors.

Draw some **witches** flying through this night sky.

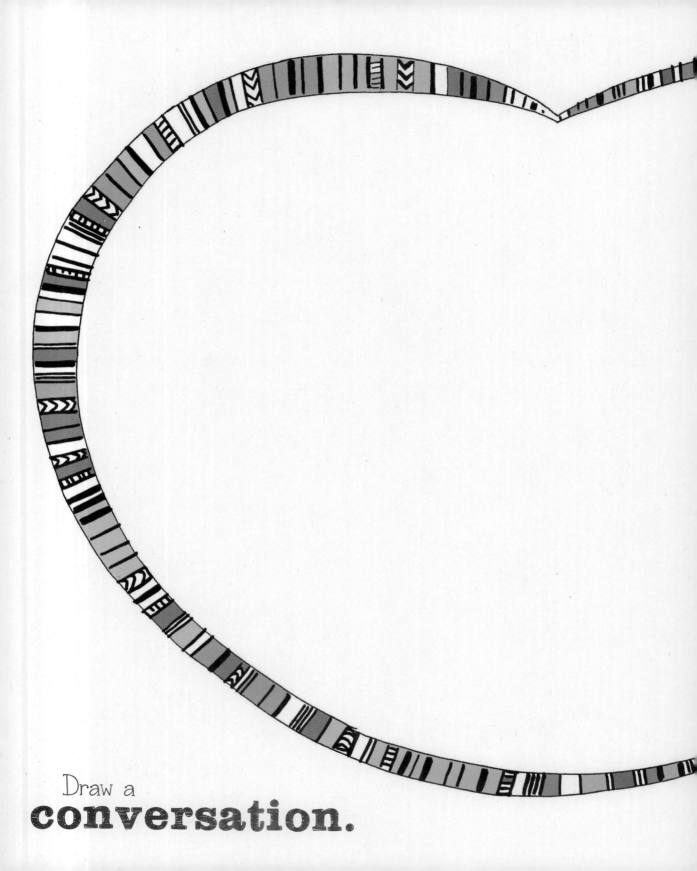

Draw a
conversation.

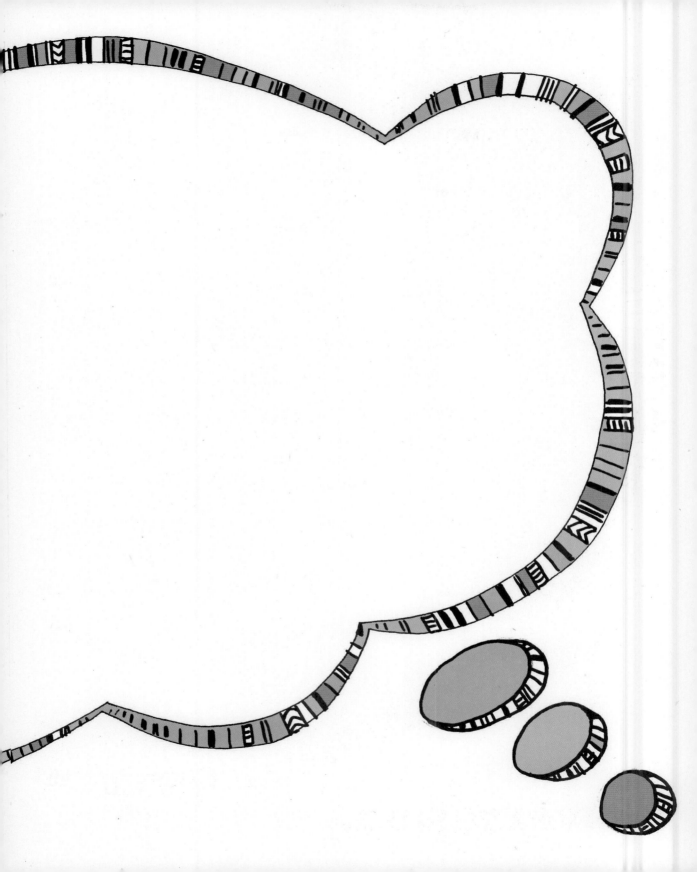

Draw a MYTH.

"Every child is an artist. The problem is how to remain an artist once we grow up."

Pablo Picasso.